The
Matron Awaits

The
Matron Awaits

by

DANNY PYLE

AVON BOOKS
1 Dovedale Studios
465 Battersea Park Road
London SW11 4LR

Printed and bound in the U.K.

Avon Books

London
First Published 1998
© Danny Pyle, 1998
ISBN 1 86033 585 3

THE NURSING HOME IN THIS SERIES DOES
NOT REPRESENT ANY REAL NURSING HOME
EITHER LIVING OR DEAD.

ALL STAFF AND OTHER PERSONNEL ARE
PURELY FICTIONAL CHARACTERS.

TO ANY PERSON BEARING ANY RESEMBLANCE
TO SAID CHARACTERS MAY WE OFFER
OUR CONDOLENCES.

CONTENTS

It Was Friday

A scream, a crash, the sound of broken crockery followed by a couple of heavier bumps sounded along the corridor.

The Matron, sitting comfortably in her office chair, had just managed to get one of her chocolates halfway to her mouth when the sound hit her eardrums. She let the chocolate fall from her fingers with surprise and hurriedly tried to get out of her chair.

She found the chair still attached to her bottom as she tried to stand up. With an action that would have done justice to a slim rumba dancer she wriggled her twenty-two stone body free of the chair and rumbled down the corridor to investigate the cause of all the noise.

What a sight met her eyes!

Milk jugs, teapots, plates, cups and saucers all smashed on the floor, and lying in a mess of spilt milk, tea and sugar was the early morning domestic, who had been taking the patients their early morning teas. Her legs were askew and showing a fair bit of thigh above her black stockings. One of her hands was still clutching the overturned trolley.

On the other side of the overturned trolley was the night nurse who, being behind schedule, had been trying to make up time as she dashed around the corner and crashed into the trolley. Her tray of medicines had gone flying and she had joined the domestic on the floor.

Nurse Peamore, as usual in the toilet, had hurriedly dressed on hearing the commotion, not realising that in her haste

she had tucked the back of her dress into her knickers thus revealing a very shapely pair of thighs.

She raced to the disaster area and promptly bounced into Matron, who had just arrived at the scene. Nurse Peamore went flying to join the pair who were already on the floor, landing face down.

Matron's body wobbled with the force of the impact, and she found she could not utter a word. Nothing like this had ever happened before in the whole of the time she had spent in the nursing service.

Young Doctor Treatemwell, who had quite a few patients to see that day, had decided to make an early start. He heard the commotion as he entered the building and dashed down the corridor to see what was happening. He had just caught a delectable view of Nurse Peamore's exposed thighs when he also crashed into Matron, lost his balance and joined the trio on the floor. Matron's body started wobbling again with this second impact, she found herself gasping for air, then fainted and fell right on top of the doctor.

Meanwhile the toast, which the early morning domestic had left in the toaster, had caught fire, causing smoke and fumes to envelope the kitchen completely. This set the fire alarms off to join the clamour of the patients ringing their bells to find out what had happened to their early morning cup of tea.

This was the scene that greeted the Assistant Matron as she entered the Nursing Home.

Seeing the alarm flashing for the kitchen area, she investigated and found the kitchen full of smoke. She promptly called the fire brigade. Then she found the mass of bodies on the floor so, ignoring for the moment all the patients' bells, she tried to roll Matron's body over and off the poor doctor, who was almost suffocating under the massive weight. And he was sure that some damage had been done to his manhood.

Somehow the Assistant Matron succeeded in freeing him and getting him to his feet. Then they both assisted the domestic, the night nurse and Nurse Peamore to their feet. Then all of them made a concerted attempt to lift the Matron, but her weight defied all their efforts. The Assistant Matron decided to fetch the gardener to come and help them, who, not being very well domesticated, came down the corridor with a load of mud still clinging to his boots. This made a right mess on the carpets.

The two men and three women had almost got Matron to her feet when the fire brigade arrived. The Assistant Matron let go her hold of Matron as she dashed to meet them. This made the others overbalance and down went the Matron again, this time pulling the doctor on top of her. As he went down his legs hit Nurse Peamore's legs causing her to lose her balance and fall on top of him.

The two that were the original cause of all this furore were the only two left standing and the sight of the tangled heap of humanity on the floor was so funny that they could do nothing but laugh and giggle at Matron flat out (if such an enormous member of the human species could be so described), Nurse Peamore lying on top of the doctor and still showing more of her anatomy than was considered respectable, the doctor himself lying on top of the Matron, feeling like a squashed sausage in a sandwich.

And beneath this pile of bodies was still the gooey mess from the original accident.

Elsewhere the firemen were being shown to the kitchen by the Assistant Matron, where it did not take them very long to have everything under control, although they did make a bit of a mess doing it.

Returning to the human heap in the corridor, the gardener, who no one had noticed disappearing, returned from his call of nature and somehow managed to get the doctor to his feet after first lifting Nurse Peamore, who immediately dashed off to the toilet. The gardener then performed a minor miracle and got Matron to her feet. She was still a bit wobbly on her pins — all this action was far more than she was used to. Normally she would spend the day directing all and sundry from her office chair, as she sat munching chocolates. She was sure she would feel better now if only she had a chocolate to munch.

The poor young doctor, suffering from delayed reaction, was doubled up in agony. He wondered if his sex life was over.

The early morning domestic and the night nurse were still in their fit of giggles. As soon as one stopped, she would look at the other and both would burst out in a fresh spate of laughter.

Matron was not pleased, in fact one could go so far as to say that she was downright angry. The gigglers would be for the high jump, along with anyone else who was responsible for this morning's fiasco. The back of Matron's uniform was covered in the gooey mess from the floor. The passageway was a mass of muddy footprints from the gardener's boots, the kitchen was in a horrible and completely unusable state, and, on top of this, she had lost her chocolate. The patients' bells were still ringing, adding to the confused state she found herself in. She felt she could not take any more and told the Assistant Matron to take over while she went home for a rest and a change of clothes.

When the rest of the day staff arrived, they found the way to the car park blocked by the fire engine, so they had to park about a quarter of a mile up the road. They were not pleased.

When the day cook arrived and saw the state of her kitchen, she nearly collapsed. It was her pride and joy, and she always kept it looking spotless. There would be no cooking today — it would take the whole day to clean up the mess. Thank goodness it was Friday. It could safely be said, that she was not pleased.

The Assistant Matron was not pleased, having to organise the disgruntled staff as they arrived. She had to send half of them out to get food for the patients from the local cafes. They were not pleased. The remaining staff had to do double the workload to cover for those that were out purchasing victuals. They were not pleased either. The domestic staff had to clean up the additional mess on top of their normal duties. They were not pleased. No one, in fact, was having a nice day.

Transport had been organised to take the doctor to hospital, where he was relieved to find that things were not as serious as he had first thought and he would still have a sex life.

Finally after a couple of hours some semblance of order seemed to emerge. The firemen had gone. The patients had all been attended to and so at last the Assistant Matron was able to start on the routine paper work.

Then there was a knock on the office door. She called out for whoever it was to enter. A medical rep came bouncing into the room with a supercilious grin on his face and asked her if she didn't get bored stiff doing such a humdrum job. He was quite amazed to find a heavy book being flung at him.

Still, it *was* Friday the thirteenth.

The First And Last Day
Of The
Holiday Relief Staff

Things started to go wrong from the very beginning of the day the holiday relief staff were taking over the kitchen.

Mindless Millie slipped on the stairs leading down to the kitchen and swore blind that someone had left a banana skin lying there. She would not admit that she was seeing double, even treble, after quite a heavy session on the hard stuff the previous evening. She had gone down with a bump and her bottom felt very sore. All the staff that entered the kitchen that morning were greeted with an explosive belch, followed by the stale smell of previously consumed alcohol. It was so strong that half the staff felt as if they themselves had been hitting the bottle.

Flopbellied Fred finally arrived, he was the other half of the holiday relief team. He looked more suited to be manning the dustcarts than seeing to the culinary requirements of the nursing home patients and staff. His face was covered in dirty grey stubble and it gave the appearance of never being in contact with soap and water. The apron he was wearing could have given competition to a Picasso abstract. Dry yellow of egg, the greeny-blue stain of cabbage juice, the pinky red of tomato ketchup and the brown remains of Daddies Sauce all helped to disguise the fact that the apron had once been white. His hands were black with grime, although for one who had done so little work and spent most of his time keeping the breweries solvent it was a mystery how they got like this. His fingernails were untrimmed, enabling them to carry a full quota of dirt.

He grunted a greeting to Mindless Millie. No apology for being late. As far as he was concerned, if he got there sometime on the correct date then he was on time.

Mindless Millie told Flopbellied Fred about her accident, so Fred put his arms around her and massaged her bottom. While he was doing this the Senior Sister entered the kitchen. She could not believe her eyes — it looked as if the holiday relief woman was having a sexy cuddle with the dustman. Reprimanding both of them, she was startled to find that the pair would be involved in the preparation and cooking of food for the staff and patients. She had to hurry away to hide the fact that she felt physically sick at the thought of these two handling food.

The boilers were turned on so there would be plenty of hot water to make tea and coffee. The only trouble with this was that neither of the relief pair thought to check how much water was in the boilers to start with. The result of this oversight was that the kitchen was filled with thick steam when Millie was trying to fry eggs. The steam was so dense and Millie was so befuddled that the eggs were cracked not only into the frying pan but over the whole stove. The porridge boiled over, making an even bigger mess, the baked beans burned and the bacon under the grill caught fire.

Flopbellied Fred managed to turn the boilers off, burning his hands in the process and treating the kitchen to language it had never heard before and probably would never hear again. By now the kitchen was covered in acrid smoke from the burning bacon and this eventually set off the automatic fire alarm.

The fire brigade arrived. Anything that had survived the steam and smoke was now smothered by foam. Even Flopbellied Fred managed to get covered in foam. He had to be hosed down and the shock of water on his skin nearly gave him a heart attack. It was much more serious than his burn. He was convinced he would catch double pneumonia when he felt fresh air on his skin.

To add to the mayhem of the morning, the patients were all ringing their bells to find out what was going on and why they were still waiting for their victuals. They were convinced that they were being starved to death so that the staff would not have the bother of looking after them. Mindless Millie was sent out to buy snacks and sandwiches. But she was a poor choice because by now all the pubs were open and suddenly Millie got this terrible thirst. It was so bad she would just have to have a quick drink before finishing her errand. But when she got to the bar, she found her old friend Gabbling Gertie so she just had to tell her about the fire. Gabbling Gertie was all agog and wanted to know all the details so, embellishing the facts a little to make the story more interesting, Millie told her the tale. Neither talker nor listener let their task interfere with their consumption of alcohol, which they were downing at a fair old rate.

Suddenly, in mid-sentence, it seemed as if Millie had been hit by a thunderbolt. She jumped up and dashed out the door. She had just remembered what she had been sent out to do.

She raced to the shops — but it was too late, it was early closing day. By now the drink she had consumed was beginning to have an effect. It would not hurt the patients to wait a bit longer, she thought, after all they had been waiting for so long that another half an hour would not make much difference. The question of where she might be able to buy the required items did not even enter her head.

Back to the pub went Millie. Gabbling Gertie was still there and had a whole crowd around her, listening to her version of the Nursing Home fire. Adding further embellishments to increase the dramatic effect on her audience:— she now had the Nursing Home burnt to the ground; the patients and staff all outside on the lawn. Some patients had been moved out whilst still in their beds. It was not known if there were any fatalities.

Mindless Millie did not know what Gabbling Gertie was going on about. Her brain could only register one thing and that was that she had to have a drink. In fact she had two or three, then had her glass refilled and went to sit down at a window seat. The strength had gone out of her and her eyes felt so sore. She thought she would just close them for a few moments' rest. A few minutes later, the crowd at the bar were treated to a loud, raucous snore and all eyes turned to see Mindless Millie out to the world.

Meanwhile, poor old Flopbellied Fred was in a bad way. In having to face the fresh air without his protective layer of dirt, he was sure he would die of the cold. He looked so pale, ill and worried he was sent home, where his wife, failing to recognise him now he was cleaned up, called the police and said she was being molested by an intruder.

The nurses had done their best to feed the patients with biscuits and snacks from their own meagre rations and had tried to give them all hot drinks, although this was a long process as they only had one small domestic kettle. No one knew what had happened to Mindless Millie. She had been gone for hours.

The Matron decided that she had had enough from this holiday relief pair. They would get their marching orders, even if it meant the nurses having to knuckle down and cook the meals for the rest of the week. When the nurses got to hear about this, they said they just would not do it.

Rumour begets rumour, so the story of the nursing home fire spread all over town, resulting in the arrival of cars and vans filled with blankets and food to clothe and feed the poor suffering patients. The drivers were amazed to see the nursing home still standing and the only visible damage a few black smudges on the exterior wall of the kitchen.

Mindless Millie was eventually found, drunk and disorderly in charge of an empty whisky bottle. She was put into custody for her own safety.

Nursing Home Battlers

Elsie Ermeltal was one of those people who knew it all and had done it all. What she herself had not done, seen or heard, members of her family had. She was the sort of person who, if there was a conversation taking place and she was not already involved, had to muscle in. Doris Seaman could not stand her. As soon as Elsie appeared Doris would start shaking with annoyance. It was like showing a red rag to a bull. It did not help matters that they both worked as cleaners in the same Nursing Home. The staff, and sometimes even the patients, would do their best to stir up bad feelings between these two, then watch from the side-lines as sparks flew.

This week there had been an unusual calm for about three days. Everyone was amazed. Was this a new dawn or was it the calm before the storm? Staff had been doing their best to stir things up but for some reason the sparks had not ignited. Even enlisting the patients to their cause had brought no success.

Then, on Thursday, it happened.

It was in the staff room at break time. Three of the nursing staff who were on the first break were talking about the drugs bust that the police had made in the town when Elsie entered the room with her cup of tea. She was a few minutes late and in a foul temper, so much so that she did not even muscle in on the conversation. She just sat down breathing heavily, her face red and her large, protruding nose seeming to quiver with anger.

It had all started at home that morning. About half an hour before the time she normally set out for work, there was a knock on her door. It was the police! They wanted a statement from her, about her daughter. When did she come home at night? What did she do during the day? Was she working and, if so, where? And a thousand and one other things ...

Elsie did not like this, people poking their nose into her family's business. Now she was getting a taste of her own medicine she did not like it one bit. She shouted at the policemen and asked what business was it of theirs what her daughter did with her time.

"We're afraid she might be mixed up in the drug scene," said one of the constables. "But if she's not, we're trying to find out. We want to establish the facts to eliminate the innocent from our enquiries."

Her daughter on drugs? Never. She was just a normal teenager. Yes, she had her moods, sometimes sulky, sometimes full of life. Yes, sometimes she screamed and shouted and swore and was awkward and did not want to do anything about the house, but all teenagers were like that nowadays weren't they?

"Anyway, I have to go to work, so you'll have to excuse me."

"Would it be more convenient to come to the station to make your statement?"

"No, it wouldn't — but I suppose I'll have to."

The police left after arranging for her to come to the station that evening.

Her daughter hadn't come home last night. This was not unusual. She often stopped at her girlfriend's house or with her boyfriend. Elsie quietly admitted to herself that she was totally out of control, but she never for one minute thought she was on drugs. And now she would be late for work. In spite of racing and tearing around, she was still late arriving for her cleaning job at the Nursing Home. She put extra muscle into her cleaning so as to vent her temper and make up for lost time, but she just ended up being late for her tea break.

Doris, who cleaned upstairs, entered with her cup of tea. Seeing Elsie on her own and not poking her nose into the conversation the nurses were having, she politely asked, with malice aforethought, if she had been sent to Coventry.

Even Doris could not have expected the reply that she got. Half a cup of hot tea was thrown at her, staining the new, clean white overall she was wearing.

Doris saw red. She flung herself at Mrs Elsie Ermeltal and tried to pull her hair out. Elsie, finding relief in action, tried to do the same to her. The three nurses cheered, egging them on, but one of them was Miss Peamore and of course she found the excitement too much and had to dash to the 'loo'.

The battle raged. Cups, saucers, books and wall charts went flying as the two pummelled and scratched one another. It only lasted about five minutes but the rest room looked like a real disaster area.

The Assistant Matron arrived and could not believe the

devastation that met her eyes. She told the nurses to get back to their duties and then questioned the two rather shame-faced cleaners, doing her best to keep a straight face as she did so.

The sight of the two cleaners was enough to bring a twinkle of amusement to anyone's eyes. Hair askew, white aprons stained and torn, blouses ripped, skirts falling; lipstick-smudged faces with evidence of scratches on both; Elsie showing a bare shoulder. The pair of them stood amongst the debris their fight had caused.

"You will both clean yourselves up and then clean up this mess. I will have to report this incident to Matron. Whether you keep your jobs or not will be up to her."

Having delivered this speech with a suitably stern face, the Assistant Matron about turned and just made it to Matron's office, where she had an attack of the giggles and finally burst into laughter as she again pictured the middle-aged women in their battle zone. Studiously avoiding one another, the two cleaners cleared up the mess. They both felt silly now, but each was convinced it was the other one's fault.

Now things were back to normal, with the two enemies at battle stations, the staff redoubled their efforts to stir it up even more.

How well they succeeded.

After the mobile patients had had their mid-day meal in the day room, they watched as the dishes were being cleared away, seemingly aware that something was about to happen. It did.

Doris accidentally trod on Elsie's foot. Elsie screamed, "You did that on purpose. You're trying to kill me."

How a trodden foot could be evidence of attempted murder defies the imagination.

"Kill you? I wouldn't dirty my hands on the likes of you, you're just a no good nosey old tart!"

That did it. They were at it again, fists flying, legs kicking, until they both lost their balance and fell to the floor. Here there was more biting and scratching, hair-pulling and clothes being torn. All of a sudden one of Elsie's plump breasts shot out, exposed for all to see. This caused many a gleam in some of the male patients' eyes but it seemed to drive Elsie crazy. She went berserk, pummelling Doris into unconsciousness.

Someone had dialled 999. Who it was was never discovered. When the police arrived on the scene Elsie was so mad she even started attacking them. After quite a tussle, they took her away and locked her in the cells.

Doris was sent to hospital, where she had a good twenty-four hours' rest. The police had taken a statement from her and asked if she wanted to press charges. She could not make up her mind so she said she still felt giddy and could they ask her again later.

At the police station, Elsie was in one cell and her daughter was in the one next to hers, having been charged with drug-dealing. Elsie knew everything about everybody else's business but did not know what was happening right under her nose in her own family.

Matron and her assistant could not help laughing at the antics of their cleaners, but it was decided they had gone too far this time. They had no option but to sack them and advertise for new cleaning staff.

The battle of the cleaners was the main topic of conversation for the rest of the week.

Staff On The Loose

Three of the nurses on the day shift were really fed up. It had been a humdinger of a week. First there was an inspection by the Health Service and the battle-axe that represented them must have got out of bed the wrong side, because there was just nothing that was to her satisfaction. Nothing pleased her. From the time of her arrival at the main entrance, where her shoe somehow became entangled in the iron grating, to the time she left and nearly went flying out the main door, as her coat caught in one of the wheelchairs and threw her off balance, she had done nothing but find fault and moan.

The result of this was that Matron was everywhere, inspecting everyone, and everything that they were doing. This meant that everyone had had to work extra hard and Matron kept the pressure on all week. The two new cleaners, who had only started that week (the previous cleaners having been sacked for fighting), wondered what sort of a place they had come to.

So the three nurses were planning a night out, when they could relax and let their hair down. Nurse Peamore, one of the nurses concerned, got so excited at the thought of a night out that she had to dash to the 'loo'. The other two nurses looked at one another. One said, "I hope she's not going to do that all the time we are out." The other replied, "Oh she will be all right, it's only this place that affects her."

The three of them were just waiting for the end of their shift so that they could rush home, wash, change and make up, ready for an evening of 'pubbin' and clubbin''. Time seemed to drag. Why was it that time spent working seemed to last forever, but free time whizzed past?

At last it was time to clock off, so the three lost no time hanging around chatting but made their various ways home to prepare for their evening's entertainment. They had arranged to meet outside the 'Dying Duck', a lively little pub near the harbour.

At seven thirty that evening they all met as planned and each one congratulated the others on their appearance. They were all rather good-looking. The dark brunette hair of Nurse Peamore set a nice contrast to the fair, blondish hair of the other two.

"Let's get sloshed," said Nurse Peamore, taking the other two by surprise. After all, she was usually the quiet and reserved one. "Let's!" said the other two in unison and away to the bar they went. They got their drinks and sat at a table not too far away from the bar, with the idea that then they would not have too far to go to get replenishments.

A little while later a huge shape darkened the pub's entrance, entered and waddled up to the bar with a diminutive little man being dragged along in tow. It couldn't be! But it was. The Matron and her husband out for a drink, and they had to pick this place. Not a very auspicious start to the evening.

Curt 'Hellos' were said and then each party ignored the other. Well, that was not quite accurate because the little man was eyeing up the nurses' legs when his wife's attention was elsewhere. When the girls noticed this somehow their dresses seemed to reveal more and more leg as they teased the little man.

Julia, the smallest of the three nurses, wondered aloud if he got seasick on top of Matron when he made love. The vision of him tossing and turning on top of Matron's mountainous sea of flesh caused all three of them to burst out laughing.

Matron looked across and smiled with her lips whilst simultaneously glaring with her eyes, as only she could do. The girls read the danger signs and thought it would be prudent to move on to pastures new. So they drank up and as they passed Matron's table curt 'Good nights' were exchanged.

They made their way to 'The Buccaneer' where music was blaring and it was crowded. The girls pushed and shoved their way to the bar. It seemed to take quite a while until they could get the barman's attention. Finally they got served and then had the problem of finding somewhere to sit. A couple of lads in RAF uniform moved up to make room for them. Julia thanked them and made sure she was the one who sat next to them. She had made up her mind, in the twinkling of an eye, that she fancied the taller of the two airmen so she did not waste any time before she got chatting to them.

Nurse Peamore thought "Here we go, them two are going to go swanning off with those airforce types and I'm going to be left here on my own." But in fact Delma, the other nurse, did not much fancy the RAF uniform. She preferred sailors, she thought they were much more romantic.

A few drinks later, mostly bought by the lads, they were all chatting away together as if they were old friends. Jokes were being exchanged and risqué stories being told. Even Nurse Peamore was relaxed and enjoying herself.

Someone suggested that they could all go on to a night-club when the pub closed. They had all had enough to drink by this time to think it was a brilliant idea, so as the bar closed they all made their way to the exit and went in search of a night-club. Turning a few corners and walking down one or two streets they came across a neon-lit doorway with a sign informing all and sundry that this was indeed a club.

Nurse Peamore was a little confused. One of the airmen had his arms around her but both of her colleagues had male arms around them. This meant there were three men, so where had the third one come from? Was she more tipsy than she realised? Actually the third man had joined them as they left the pub but Nurse Peamore had been so interested in what her new friend was telling her that she hadn't noticed the increase in their numbers.

After a little bit of bargaining with the doorman they gained entry to the club. In the subdued lighting they made their way to a table after being served drinks. They had all enjoyed themselves up to now and the evening carried on being pleasant as all three couples got up to dance. Nurse Peamore was with the tall, good-looking airman, Julia with the shorter one, and Delma had settled for the man in civvies. After a few turns on the dance floor they returned to the table and had a few more drinks. That's when Nurse Peamore found out that the man in civvies had also been in the Royal Air Force but had been demobbed two weeks previously.

It was now in the early hours of the morning and the night-club was closing so they all made their way to the fresh air. When the fresh air hit them it really made their legs wobble. After a little bit of horse play they regained a semblance of control over their limbs and started on their way. A catlike caterwauling issued forth from them, which in their drunken state they fondly thought was singing.

A policeman materialized before them and asked them to keep the noise down, and for this friendly request he had his hat knocked off and kicked about like a football. The six of them then ran down the road with his helmet in their possession. He chased after them for a little way but stopped when he saw they had left his helmet lying in the road. The arm of the law did not think it worth stretching after them. If he had done so there would not have been so many dustbins upturned with the contents strewn all over the road, so many red traffic cones in among the flower beds, so many signposts turned around the wrong way. Various other acts of vandalism were perpetrated and the high jinks only stopped when they arrived at Nurse Peamore's flat.

After a struggle to get the key in the lock they finally managed to open the door. When they were inside one of the lads produced a bottle of whisky. As Nurse Peamore did not have enough glasses for everyone it was arranged that the girls had the glasses while the men drank from cups.

Music was played as the night progressed, marathon snogging sessions and more taking place. Nurse Peamore insisted it was her right as party host to have a snogging session with each of the male members of the party (and she was supposed to be the quiet one). It was a great night and everyone was having a fabulous time, as attested by the laughter and shrieks of enjoyment, when, suddenly, Nurse Peamore passed out.

This sort of brought an end to the party. The girls with a bit of a struggle undressed her (not that she was still wearing many items of clothing) and put her to bed. The tall airforce lad said he would stay with her to see that she was all right. Everyone thought this was a great idea and then had another. They put something beside the bed with a note attached.

The four then left the flat, not realising or caring that they were minus several items of clothing. These were strewn all over the flat, making it look as if an orgy of Roman proportions had taken place. The flat was left in chaos.

Delma was the only one on duty the next day and then not until the late shift. Perhaps this was just as well in the circumstances for none of the girls was in a fit state to go to work the next morning. Delma found the room going around in circles when she woke up and vowed never again to go on the drink. It is doubtful that this vow will be kept. Julia had the biggest hangover in her life and wished she were dead.

And as for Nurse Peamore, she woke up in a rather befuddled state and could not understand how she could be awake and still snoring. It then dawned on her that she was not alone in her bed. Her mind did a flashback to the night before and she remembered they had all come back to her flat. Then everything had gone blank, although she dimly remembered her friends putting her to bed with a lot of horseplay and giggling. Then she had dreamt that she was on an ocean liner with this super sort of guy and they were making love in a cabin, the action enhanced by the gentle roll of the ship. It had been a beautiful dream.

"My God!" she yelled, as it dawned on her that the lovemaking had been real even if the ocean liner was not. She shot out of bed, tripping over her little niece's toy pram. There was a note attached to it: "IN CASE YOU DID NOT TAKE PRECAUTIONS."

THE NIGHT STAFF

It is noticeable that people who are constantly employed on night work seem to have a pronounced yellow pallor. By the end of this night the pallor of the night shift would be even more noticeable.

There were three on graveyard duty, one sister and two nurses. Sister Dauntsey was of the old school. She believed in discipline. She always addressed the staff by their surnames and did not agree with all this informality that seemed to be creeping in everywhere. Her nickname (never used within earshot) was Sister Jackboots. One of the reasons for this was because of the way she walked, back ramrod straight. She marched rather than walked as she went about her duties. Another reason was her dictatorial attitude toward staff and patients. She practically had the patients sitting to attention in bed! Everyone had to do what she said, when she said — or else! A mistake, even a minor one, brought forth a torrent of abuse and a lecture on how efficiency was of paramount importance in life. Needless to say Sister Dauntsey was feared by both staff and patients.

This had been a bad day for Sister (Jackboots) Dauntsey. She had been in an argument at the supermarket with the check-out girl, insisting that she had been overcharged. A flaming row developed between her and the woman behind her in the queue who was in a hurry to get home and cook her husband's supper. She did not get any reduction in her bill and left in a furious temper.

Coming to work she had been unable to park in the staff

car park because workmen were laying new drains and had dug trenches everywhere. She parked her car outside a residence across the road from the nursing home. The owner of this residence came flying out of her gate and told the sister to move her car as she was not allowed to park there. Now Sister Dauntsey had just about had enough so she merely gave the woman a two-fingered salute and was just about to get out of the car when the woman opened the door on the other side and jumped in. Sister Dauntsey was surprised by this on two counts. One, it was most unusual for her to leave the side door unlocked and two, people did not behave like this.

"Remove this car from the front of my house, or I will stay in here all night," said the intruder. Her eyes were popping out of her head. She appeared to be quite mad and capable of doing anything.

Sister Dauntsey decided that the best way to deal with this lunatic was to take her straight to the police station. This she did, but at the police station she had another argument, this time with the desk sergeant. It was obvious she got right up the sergeant's nose. He informed her that it was a domestic affair and he could do nothing about it. He insisted that Sister Dauntsey must take the woman back to her house or she, Sister Dauntsey, would be charged with abduction. What was the world coming to? thought Sister Dauntsey. Those that tried to uphold the law were punished while those that flouted it seemed to be protected.

To be on the safe side she returned to the street where the woman lived, parking quite a distance from her house, so the woman would have a fair distance to walk. As soon as the woman got out of the car Sister Dauntsey sped off until she was outside the same house again. She parked and made sure all the doors were locked. This helped ease her discontent a little and she gave a quiet little smirk to the night at large.

Of course the incident had made her quite late for duty.

This caused another argument with the senior nurse she was taking over from.

Of the two nurses on duty, Nurse Prendegast was the complete opposite of the nursing sister. She was a pretty, demure human being who wanted to please and help everyone. As a consequence she got treated like a doormat, everyone walked all over her. She became more nervous and more unsure of herself every night she spent on duty with Sister Dauntsey.

The other nurse was Nurse Goldman, who had two main interests in life, men and money, in either order. When she was short of either of these commodities she spent her time dreaming about them. She hated working with Sister Dauntsey because when she was on duty there was no time to spare dreaming of her two favourite topics. She was not bad looking, in a plain sort of way, with a nice, well-rounded figure. She was jealous of Nurse Prendegast's good looks, but despised her nervous and unsure manner, which seemed to be getting worse each night.

Sister Dauntsey despised the two young nurses and thought they were the worst pair she had ever had to work with. She felt that if she were not on duty there, the nursing home patients would be in dire trouble. Those were the three night staff on duty.

Pills and other medicaments had been dispensed and all the patients had had their needs attended to. Now it was time for the staff's first break, when Sister (Jackboots) Dauntsey expected to have a cooked supper prepared for her by her underlings. She then generously allowed them to sit with her and have a snack and a cup of tea.

They were all sitting down, partaking of their meal. It was midnight. All three of them heard this strange tapping at the window. Their heads turned in unison and the sight that met their eyes was really appalling. A head that seemed half human and half animal glared through the window at them. The yellow eyes of the creature shone with hatred and malice, and a cloven hoof was tapping.

Fear went through the three staff like a bolt of lightning. They jumped up from their chairs and huddled together in fright. Sister Dauntsey felt more afraid and uncertain than she had ever felt in her life. Forgetting her position as the one in charge, she clung to the other two.

As suddenly as it had appeared the apparition at the window vanished, but this did not ease the tension. Into that room came such a feeling of horror, hatred and malice that the poor humans present felt as if they were being crushed into another dimension. One of intense evil.

Then a strange thing happened. Nurse Prendegast felt an overwhelming love for Sister Dauntsey and was jealous of the other nurse clinging to her. She roughly pushed Nurse Goldman away and threw her arms around the sister. Their lips met in a kiss of unbridled passion. Sister Dauntsey melted in a sea of love and wanted nothing more than to have and receive the love of Nurse Prendegast. She would do anything for her. Nurse Goldman looked on in amazement. Then she had this impulsive urge to take off her clothes and dance. None of them saw the now laughing face of the horrible monstrosity return to the window.

Nurse Prendegast gently removed all the clothes from Sister Dauntsey, who submissively helped her. She wanted to be naked to give her full love to Nurse Prendegast (it was awful but she could not recall her first name). Nurse Prendegast then stripped off all her own clothes in a frenzied hurry. Nurse Goldman felt excited as she watched them and her dancing became even more erotic. The apparition at the window cackled with laughter.

The roaring of the banshee was in everyone's ears and it drove them wild. The pair entwined their bodies and they made love with lustful abandon. Nurse Goldman was not going to be left out. She joined them and then it was just a seething mass of arms, legs, breasts, bottoms and faces in all and every which way. The more abandoned they became the stronger the evil in that room grew. Yet the patients heard nothing and slept with the innocent sleep of the untarnished.

Suddenly, in front of Sister Dauntsey, the face of Nurse Prendegast changed and it was the face of the old woman who had argued about the sister's car being parked in front of her house. The face laughed and cackled, as the sister, naked and unprotected in any way, felt drawn into the deepest depths of despair. She pushed the body away from her in revulsion.

Nurse Prendegast was hurt. The person for whom she felt the deepest love had pushed her away. Then her love became mixed up with hatred and she wanted to hurt the Sister and make her feel pain, as she felt pain in her heart. She punched and pummelled Sister Dauntsey black and blue.

The other woman could not retaliate, she could not even move. She was petrified. She thought she was being kicked by the cloven hoofs of the beast at the window Nurse Goldman meanwhile was enjoying the greatest thrill of her life. She was being pummelled this way and that between the other two women, who did she but know it had no awareness that she was even there.

Suddenly the noise of the banshee stopped. The evil that had permeated that room disappeared. The three, extremely embarrassed, naked, blushed with shame at what they had done. They dressed without speaking to one another.

The rest of the night shift was completed in almost complete silence. Every time their paths crossed in the line of duty, they blushed profusely. None of them realised that a bit of evil had entered their beings and life would never be quite the same again.

When they arrived to take over, the day staff were amazed at the change in each woman. Sister Dauntsey had a very grey pallor and seemed so uncertain about what she had to do. Nurse Prendegast had also altered. She was now extremely sure of herself, even if she also had this grey pallor. She helped Sister Dauntsey to her car. And Nurse Goldman was drained. All she wanted to do was to go home and rest, there was hardly any life left in her. She also wore this grey look.

The old lady who had argued about the car was found dead at the bottom of her stairs. Her neck was broken. There were many items of black magic regalia found at her home.

The Matron's Diet

Matron was enjoying a nice bath at home. She was quite happy and relaxed until she tried to get out and found herself wedged firmly in the tub. When with all her heaving, shoving and pushing she found she could not dislodge herself, she began to get worried. She called out to her husband, although what a seven stone weakling could do to shift a twenty-two stone woman was a matter for conjecture.

Her husband was downstairs watching a football match on the telly and at the very moment his wife called out, a goal had been scored and the roar from the crowd had drowned out her cries for help. Blissfully unaware of the drama upstairs, the husband continued to watch the football match until, during a lull in the game, a voice bellowed, so loudly that the whole building seem to shake, "Help me!"

Suppose she wants me to pass her the towel, he muttered angrily to himself. He seldom got much peace when she was at home. Still, he knew better than to ignore her. So off he went, trooping up the stairs, knowing for a fact that goals would be scored during his absence.

In the bathroom, the bath filled to overflowing with the mountain of flesh that was his wife, he asked what she wanted.

"I can't get out!" she sobbed.

He had an irrational thought about how the water couldn't get in. He grabbed her hands and tried to pull, making as much impression as a dog's flea biting an elephant.

After ten minutes of useless shoving and pulling, he stopped, sweating and feeling exhausted.

"It's no good, my dear," he said. "We'll have to get some outside help. I'll go and call the doctor."

Matron blushed at the thought of the doctor seeing her stuck in the bath like this. He was a doctor, so the sight of a naked body would be nothing new to him, but it was still very embarrassing.

The doctor arrived. He and the husband tried to dislodge Matron, but it was no good. The doctor said there was nothing for it but to call in the fire brigade.

The fire brigade arrived a short while later and sorted out the problem by using hydraulic lifting gear. Matron's face was now a beetroot red with embarrassment at all the firemen seeing her in her birthday suit and seeing how her weight had trapped her in the bath. It did not help her feel any better when she heard them cracking jokes about human elephants.

The firemen left and the doctor insisted Matron should go to bed where he gave her a check-up. As was to be expected, her heart was beating too fast and her poor physical condition did not help matters.

"I'm afraid you will have to go on a strict diet from now on. You must lose weight or you could be in very serious trouble," advised the doctor. Being in a state of turmoil from her ordeal in the bath, followed by the embarrassment of all those people seeing her in the nude with her rolls of flesh there in plain sight for all to see, she meekly agreed, and really meant it.

The next morning she had black, sugarless coffee and one piece of dry toast for breakfast. The husband sat goggle-eyed in amazement. He had never thought he would see the day when she actually would start dieting. So many times she had said that she was going to go on a diet, starting the next day, but when the day dawned she had lost the enthusiasm to start. Her will power in this respect was very weak. So when she actually started dieting the shock to her husband was severe. But she had been quite shaken up with what had happened to her yesterday and had finally decided she really must do something about her weight.

At work she caused quite a few surprises. There was no morning box of chocolates. All the hot drinks she had contained no milk or sugar, but the biggest surprise of all was that she did not spend the day in her office chair. This resulted in one or two of the staff, who were inclined to take things easy and let others do the work, being caught out. Matron was able to release some of her pent-up feelings by giving them a right tongue-lashing. The word soon spread, and it was surprising how everyone seemed to become much more efficient and took much more care over their various tasks. Matron, enjoying this new found energy, was everywhere. She managed to find fault with everyone about something or other. The staff swear that when she went off duty that day the building itself gave a sigh of relief.

As soon as she got home, Matron had to soak her feet in cold water. They were sore and uncomfortable after having the unaccustomed task of supporting her body for such long periods. Her husband came home from work, wondering how long her diet had lasted. He received quite a shock when he found she was still on it. All she had for dinner was a small portion of poached fish, one small boiled potato and a few leaves of lettuce. For dessert she just had an apple. She even helped with the washing up. He began to get enthusiastic about this diet. There were unexpected perks.

Later that evening, after resting her feet some more, she said that she felt like going out for a walk. This would enable her to burn up a few more calories. Her husband would have preferred to stay home and watch the telly but he knew she would not allow him to do this. As well as perks there were some snags with her being on a diet.

They made an odd couple walking along, more like mother and son than man and wife. He asked if she would like a beer or something at the pub. She said she most certainly would not, she was trying to lose weight not put it on. Pity really because he just fancied a beer. Finishing their walk they went home and were early to bed.

The next morning Matron woke up in a foul mood. She felt so uneasy and very short-tempered. She snapped at her husband without just cause. At work she became a fiery dragon, breathing fire at anyone unlucky enough to cross her path. With her medical training she should have recognised the withdrawal symptoms being caused by her diet.

Then something happened that upset her even more.

She had just finished telling off one of the cleaners for some shoddy cleaning work when the cleaner said she hoped she enjoyed her bath, in a quite sarcastic tone. Matron turned scarlet and asked what she meant. The cleaner answered, "My husband is a fireman and he helped you with the hydraulic lift." Matron had hoped to be able to keep her ordeal from being known at her place of work. She now realised this was a forlorn hope.

Now her job would be extremely difficult. She would have to treat that cleaner with kid gloves and trust she would not tell the rest of the staff. This also proved a forlorn hope.

No one said anything to Matron — no one dared — but the sniggering in odd corners and the look of amusement in the staff's eyes gave away the fact that her bath ordeal had become common knowledge. Now everyone knew what had caused her to go on a diet.

Her temper became worse as the days went by. Her face took on a haggard look as she lost weight. It would have been better if she had been able to lose weight in the right places.

Three weeks passed, and now she was much happier as her body adjusted to the new regime. She had been amazed at herself for being able to keep to the diet for so long. She now had no craving for chocolate. In fact, she thought the taste she could remember was horrible and could not understand why she had liked it so much. Now her taste buds were not numbed by all the chocolate she use to eat, she could taste the long-forgotten flavours of fresh food.

In the first week of the diet she had lost quite a bit of weight, but the second week had been a little disappointing. The doctor had said this was quite normal. This had eased her mind and the remaining tension had disappeared. Now she was losing a little weight each week and she found she did not get tired so quickly. She started to enjoy life again, she seemed to have more energy to burn up than she had had for a very long time.

The one who suffered most from this state of affairs was her husband. Her sexual demands upon him increased more and more. She seemed to be insatiable. He became such a physical wreck of a man that the doctor had to put him on a diet to increase his weight and build up his strength.

The Happening

It had been a long, hot summer but now the weather had turned — after all it was November. It had been a proper November day, the rain had fallen from a dark and dismal sky. It had not stopped all day, just one long, continuous downpour. Now as evening turned into night, the wind rose, shrieking in anger. It was a cold, biting wind that penetrated right through to one's bones. Nurse Allison Markett shivered. She was so relieved when she was inside the nursing home, out of the pouring rain and biting wind and the warmth of the building was causing steam to rise from her sodden clothing. She was the last of the night staff to arrive. The other three had entered a few minutes before her, long enough to get a brew going. She gratefully accepted a nice hot cup of tea.

Sister Becket was the night sister in charge of the nursing home. She had a round, happy face which reflected her warm and happy personality. She was unlike the sister she had taken over from as could be. Her predecessor had retired with ill health. There were rumours that something awful had happened on her last night of duty. Now Sister (Jackboots) Dauntsey was no longer at the nursing home the atmosphere was quite friendly.

Everyone loved working with Sister Becket. All the jobs seemed to get done in a smooth and efficient manner with no hassle. It was Sister Becket who introduced the idea that the staff should start their duty with a cup of tea or coffee and a little natter together. Thus any gossip was got rid of right at the beginning of the shift and all could concentrate on their duties. This also fostered the team spirit.

Nurse Ellen Drew was also on duty, a really attractive girl, with long, glistening chestnut-brown hair, blue eyes and a perky little turned-up nose. She was not tall but her body was so well proportioned that her movements were sheer poetry in motion.

Nurse Sheila Maureen Butte completed the foursome. Her features were more of the motherly type. She had a friendly, homely face with kind eyes and a ready smile. She was a little on the plump side.

Together they made a good, hard working team that made the patients feel they were in good hands.

Outside the wind howled and the rain lashed against the windows. "It seems to be getting worse," commented Sister Becket.

"Hope it clears up by the time our shift is finished," said Nurse Butte. The others all murmured agreement. They all hoped the rain would have spent itself and they could make their way home in the dry.

"Well, it's time we got started," said Sister Becket. "The sooner we get working, the faster the time will go."

Everyone agreed with Sister and set about their various tasks. After two hours of duty it was time for their midnight break. It was possible for all of them to have their break at the same time on the night shift, unlike the day shift when split breaks had to be taken. The tea had been brewed and snacks were on the table as all four sat down together.

There had been a new admission since the previous night. A Mr George Tumbrill had been put in room fourteen. He was an ageing skeleton of a man who did not seem long for this world. They wondered about him, as they ate their food, with the natural curiosity of the female species.

The rain seemed to lash with even greater strength against the windows, while the wind, not to be outdone, increased its ferocity. It really was a stormy night. They were all thankful to be indoors, warm and dry.

Suddenly all the lights went out! As they became accustomed to the darkness they could just make out the windows and the walls. Then a peculiar light, a greyish, misty sort of light, covered the whole room with an ethereal glow, and there was almost complete silence. Neither the wind nor the rain could be heard. But there was the sound of someone sighing, sighing as if they could not be bothered to go on living.

The ground beneath them became green fields. There was a man walking his dog. It was all so peaceful the four nursing staff were entranced, not afraid. The man was remarkably well built and his springy step matched the bouncy energy of his Old English sheepdog. The kinship between the two was obvious. Happiness emanated from them both. Some of the fields were covered in buttercups, others were decorated with daisies. The horizon was the grey mist.

After a time the man gradually faded away into the grey mist, led by the dog. Then for a moment he came back through the mist, facing them. A smile of peace and contentment was on his face. It was a full and healthy face and, but for that fact, it would have been identical to that of George Tumbrill, the man in room fourteen. The face faded away again, then the fields disappeared and the mist evaporated.

The lights came back on, the wind and rain could be heard again. The four staff looked at one another in amazement. Such a strange experience had never happened to any of them before. But no fear had been felt, just an immense feeling of peace. They still felt at peace, but puzzled by what had happened. Although it seemed that they had been in this situation for an age, hardly any time had elapsed at all.

For a time they all felt as if they could not speak of this event. It seemed as if they were bound by some unseen force to meditate inwardly, keeping their thoughts to themselves. After a little while this force seem to leave them, allowing them to talk of their experience.

Nurse Butte was the first to speak. "Did you see that man's face? He was just like that man in room fourteen, only younger."

"Did you see that beautiful sheepdog?" asked Sister Becket.

"The pastures — do you think we had a preview of heaven?" queried Nurse Drew. "Everything was so peaceful."

"What was it we saw? Was it an hallucination? If it was, how come we all saw it at the same time?" These questions were put by Nurse Markett.

They discussed the problem, if such it could be called, as they had a final fresh brew of tea before going back to their duties. Nothing could be solved. All one could say was, that there had been a 'happening'.

The rest of the shift was uneventful, apart from the fact

that Mr George Tumbrill was found dead in his bed at six a.m. On his bed and on the mat beside his bed there were dog hairs. This was unusual because no dogs were allowed in the nursing home. Dog hairs were also found in the staff rest room! The day staff, when they were told about the 'happening', thought it was a cock and bull story made up by the night staff to cover the fact that they had had a dog on the premises during their tour of duty.

Later it was discovered that Mr Tumbrill had owned an Old English sheepdog. It had died two weeks before his death. Had the dog come to lead his master to pastures new? Is this what the night staff had seen in their 'happening'. Who can say? We only know of this dimension, but that is not to say there are not other dimensions, of which some are privileged to be given a sighting.

THE DAY THE MEDICINES GOT MIXED UP

Nurse Featheringley was in love and it showed. She went about her duties with a faraway look in her eyes, oblivious of people around her, and did not answer when spoken to, or if she did answer the reply she gave made no sense. Her mind was not on her job as she automatically went about her duties. All she could really think about was being in her loved one's arms, and how her whole body seemed to melt to jelly when he held her. Dreamily she went from one chore to the next almost unaware of what she was doing. The rest of the staff exchanged nudges and winks when they saw the state she was in. They also tried a little teasing, but this had no effect because of her trance-like state.

Everything seemed to be going on reasonably smoothly in the nursing home. Breakfast had been served, dishes cleared away, patients had been washed and their various needs seen to. The medicines had been given out by the nurses to the patients in their charge. Then within half an hour the peace and tranquillity was brought to an abrupt end.

Two of Nurse Featheringley's patients were zooming around the corridors in their wheelchairs, no doubt imagining themselves on a racing circuit. While they were enjoying themselves in this manner the existence of many vases and other bric-a-brac was brought to an abrupt end, at least as compete objects. The smashed bits of crockery peppered the corridor, but this did not deter the speeding oldsters. They were also bumping into many of the staff and speeding away before they could be caught. Another of Nurse

Featheringley's patients (male) was trying to get into another (female) patient's bed and almost but not quite succeeding. Having one leg in plaster and one of his arms swathed in bandages made this feat just not quite possible.

There were further disruptions to the peace and tranquillity of this normally well-run nursing home. Prim and proper patient Pauline Perrywinkle, usually one of the most quiet and retiring sort, was now behaving in a way that one would never have thought possible. She was arguing with an assistant nurse, trying to get her uniform off, claiming the uniform belonged to her as she was actually the nurse and the assistant nurse was really the patient. The assistant nurse had no idea how to cope with this situation. Just at that moment the two madcap wheelchair drivers came hurtling around the corner, chortling with delight. They were being chased by the cleaners, assistant nurses and nurses, and trundling up in the rear came Matron. The argument between patient Pauline Perrywinkle and the assistant nurse stopped as they both watched goggle eyed in amazement as the parade zoomed past. Pauline Perrywinkle doubled up with laughter. Totally gone was the butter-wouldn't-melt-in-my-mouth type that she normally was.

Matron was wondering what had happened to her usually staid and efficient nursing home. At the moment it was more like a lunatic asylum. And she was not the only one meditating on the cause of the patients unusual behaviour. The whole staff — with the exception of one — were bewildered.

The one exception was the nurse whose head was up in the clouds. All she could think about was the lover who would be waiting for her when she came off duty. She was in such a bemused state she was totally unaware of what was going on around her. Coming around a corner she bumped into Matron, who was still at the tail end of those chasing the wheelchair speedsters. Now, although Matron was no longer the twenty-two and a half stone that she had once been, she was still a hefty person to bump into. In a stentorian voice (sergeant major parade-ground style) she demanded of Nurse Featheringley whether she were blind or drunk, or had been taking pills or something. Or was there some other reason for going about one's duty with the glazed eye of a moron?

This short but sharp lambasting from Matron had the desired effect of waking her from her stupor and returning her to the world of nursing. She informed Matron that she had not been taking pills or drugs and she was neither drunk or blind.

"Then what is wrong with you, nurse? You are going around like a lovesick swan."

How Matron knew what a lovesick swan looked like is a matter for conjecture. Actually it was a pretty apt description of Nurse Featheringley. Matron continued with a brisk lecture.

"When you are here nurse, you must be professional about your duties. You must be alert at all times and help me to run a well-organised and peaceful nursing home where the patients can relax and enjoy their mature years. You must keep your private and professional life separate."

"Yes Matron, I will, I'm sorry," said Nurse Featheringley meekly. Meanwhile the patients were still causing mayhem in the well-run nursing home. Betty Boothroyd, eighty-five years old, was riding up and down in the chairlift yelling "Yippee!" It was almost as good as the rides she used to get at the fairground when she was a teenager, alas so many years ago. At last one of the racing wheelchairists had been caught and put to bed, where he immediately fell asleep. His snoring could be heard the full length of the corridor. But three other patients were chucking the books around in the day room. They were playing throw and catch but very few catches were made so the floor became littered with literature. After a struggle the staff got these three old vandals and put them back in their separate rooms. By now Betty Boothroyd had had enough of the chairlift. She was beginning to feel quite tired so she meekly let the staff put her to bed. That evening she ate all her food and even asked for more. This was most unusual as she normally only pecked at her food leaving most of it uneaten.

Now all the staff could concentrate on catching the wheelchair speedster. He was having the time of his life as he eluded capture. The more they chased him, the more he enjoyed it. But whizzing around a corner, with the staff in hot pursuit, he was unlucky enough to knock down the ageing doctor who had just entered the building. The doctor had to be rushed to hospital. Finding all attention diverted away from him, the patient got worried about what he had done and quietly made his way back to his own room.

Pauline Perrywinkle had now given up the idea that she was a nurse and had wandered outside into the garden, where she became convinced she was the gardener. She started pulling out all the yellow flowers, muttering to herself, "How these yellow weeds spread everywhere." When the real gardener arrived and saw what she had done to his flower-beds, he went purple with rage and stormed into Matron's office — unfortunately, just as the girl with the staff hot drinks was coming out. There was a collision of bodies, the tray went flying into the air and hot tea rained down, mostly on the gardener. This did not help his temper. Matron and the nurse who attended to his burns had to listen to his cursing and swearing as they did their best to ease his pain. They were informed, with the help of colourful expletives, how it had taken weeks of hard work to get the flower-beds just right. As soon as the work was completed along came a vandal who ruined everything.

They went outside on his insistence to have a look at his ruined flower-beds. Betty Boothroyd was still there, she must have been just behind the shed when the gardener first saw the damage. He had gone to Matron's office without doing a full inspection, thinking the damage must have been done the previous evening. When Matron saw the vandal was none other than Betty, she coaxed her into her office and asked her why she had done this.

"It's my job," said Betty, "I'm the gardener and I am only pulling out the weeds."

Seeing that she could not get any sense out of the patient, Matron got the nurse to put her to bed, and then put her hands up to her face. "Whatever else is going to happen? It's more like a lunatic asylum than a nursing home!"

When things had settled down to almost normal, Matron called a staff meeting to try and find out why the patients were acting so abnormally. Eventually the cause of all the upset was found. Nurse Featheringley had mixed up the medicines and given the wrong items to her patients. Hers had been the only patients to cause all the mayhem. Nurse Featheringley almost got the sack.

Was it the wrong medicines though? It had done the patients the world of good. The only real casualties had been the doctor, the gardener and the flower-beds. All made full recoveries.

THE HAUNTED ROOM

Sister Becket, the most popular sister that had ever been on nights in the nursing home, had been seriously injured in a car accident. All the staff had been quite shocked when they heard of this. It was unlikely that she would ever recover sufficiently to be able to return to duty.

Her replacement, Sister Henrietta Fortesque, could not be more different. Her face was carved in granite, she demanded obedience and respect from the night staff. Her word was law. The night staff felt that they were in a different place of employment, the atmosphere was so strange and hostile.

The cosy camaraderie of the first cuppa together was the first thing to end. Sister Henrietta Fortesque had to have coffee served to her, in her office before anyone could attend to the comforts of the staff of the lower ranks.

She made it plain that she intended spending the majority of her time on duty, in the office. (Shades of what Matron used to be like.) She said she would come down like a ton of bricks on anyone not doing their job properly. Sister Becket had never felt the need to make any such statement but the work had still been done and in a most satisfactory manner. The staff hoped that after the first week, the new sister would relax a little in her manner toward them but the opposite was the case. Everyone who worked on nights detested her but feared her ferocity so the work was done well but with an undercurrent of resentment.

Two weeks later Sister Becket took a turn for the worse

and did not recover. Her funeral was attended by all the staff except for the skeleton crew left to manage the nursing home.

In the home all the rooms were full apart from room fourteen. It was situated well away from the other rooms, being at the end of a long corridor. It even had its own fire exit.

One night, a few weeks after Sister Becket's funeral, moans and groans were heard along the corridor leading to room fourteen. This was dutifully reported to the Night Sister, and Sister Fortesque told the staff they must be imagining things, but she had gone a shade paler when the staff reported this. She said that, just to be on the safe side, no one was to go near room fourteen. She would have a look on her own a little later, but no one else was to go near there. It was unlike her to be concerned for the staff or to repeat herself like this. It was also unlike her to leave her office to wander around the home. The night staff wondered if she was mellowing, just a little.

The keys to number fourteen were kept in the office. All unoccupied rooms were kept locked. Sister Fortesque did go down to the corridor of room fourteen but she did not open the room. Later she called all the staff together to tell them that she had investigated the room but could find no reason for the noises heard although it had been extremely cold in there. She again stressed that no other staff should go near there.

The staff willingly obeyed her. It was creepy enough working in the occupied part of the building without wandering to the dark and empty part.

Word spread that room fourteen was haunted. Moans, groans and sighs had been heard on many nights. Some said it was Sister Becket, who was disappointed by the way her replacement acted toward the staff and had come back to haunt the place. Fantastic as this idea was, it took root and was embellished by the staff, although not in the hearing of the night sister.

Eventually these rumours did reach the ears of Sister Granite Face as she was unaffectionately known. Instead of ridiculing them as one might have expected, she encouraged the staff to think it was haunted. This was not done in any direct manner, but by way of subtle hints dropped on various occasions — saying how cold it always was in the room in question; how sometimes she could sense another presence there; the evil that could almost be felt when one entered the door of room fourteen — and many other gentle hints, strong enough to warn anyone to keep away.

Sister Henrietta Fortesque received a good salary for her duties as night sister, but she was one of those persons who could never have enough, she always wanted more. She was not too fussy about how she made it, although she would never deal in drugs.

Her friend, Mr Silas Phillips, who had businesses in both London and Birmingham, was one of her extra sources of income. It had happened like this. He had once come to her with a problem which she had been able to solve, and for this she received regular payments. Mr Silas Phillips, himself married, had been carrying on an affair with a married woman and it had got to a pitch where they had to see more of each other, but did not know how to do this without making their spouses suspicious. The answer to this problem had been provided by Sister Fortesque. She had suggested that his woman friend could pretend to be working part-time on nights at the nursing home. If anyone phoned during the night, the night sister would take the call and cover for her. He could always be in London or Birmingham on business as far as his wife was concerned. (If only he knew — his wife could not have cared less where he was. She was having an affair of her own. The more he was away, the more she could indulge.)

One late evening Mr Phillips was leaving a hotel with his girl-friend when he almost bumped into a business acquaintance. He was able to whisk his girl around the corner before they were spotted. He broke out in a cold sweat. It would have been a disaster to have been seen by the man, who was a regular visitor to his home. This really shook him up and he realised that it was too risky to go on using the hotels.

When he next saw Sister Fortesque he mentioned this problem to her. She said she had an idea, but it would cost him quite a bit, because she risked losing everything if she was caught. A quite substantial sum of money changed hands. The granite features of the sister almost broke out into a smile. Only the power of money could do this. She then outlined her plan to him. He thought it was great, there would be one or two minor problems but nothing that could not be overcome.

Three nights later Mr Phillips and his mistress were let into the nursing home through the fire door near room fourteen by the night sister. Opening the door to room fourteen she let them both inside and then locked them in, as she said, for both her safety and theirs. She would let them out when it was safe, in the early hours of the morning when the night staff were occupied elsewhere. That was the first night when moans, groans and sighs had been heard.

When this had been reported to the night sister she had felt her heart do a somersault. This was why she had gone pale. She had been almost found out before she could collect the rent for the room for next time. She then saw that, provided she could keep everyone from going near room fourteen, there was no need to bring her new income to an end. Therefore, as before stated, she played on the natural fear of the night staff personnel.

The next morning, letting the couple out, she asked them to be a little quieter next time. The woman said she was sorry but she could not help herself when she became excited.

The arrangement, using room fourteen once, twice,

sometimes even three times, a week would have gone on indefinitely if one night something very frightening had not occurred. The pair of them had been locked in and they had stripped for their night of passion when they were shaken to the very marrow of their bones. Floating through the walls was a grey mist, which formed into the shape of a woman. This woman or apparition had a chubby face with a great sadness in her eyes. Then she was gone. The naked pair cuddled together in fright — there was such a coldness in that room. Then their clothes started floating about in the air. The pair could hardly breathe for fright, and neither could speak. The clothes finally came to rest. The pair tried to dress, shivering from fear and the intense cold. Their hands fumbling with straps and buttons, it took them quite a time to complete their task. They had both lost all interest in sex, all they wanted to do was to get out of there. They clung together in fear, for there was no way out until the sister came to unlock the door for them. They had to stay prisoners inside the room which was more like a cell after the ghostly visit. This played on both their minds. The lady of the grey mist did not reappear but this did not lessen the terror they both felt.

The mistress pleaded with her lover to break down the door so they could both escape but he could not do this. He could not endanger the sister after all she had done for him. Besides, he had an idea that she could be very vindictive if crossed. The ghost was the lesser of the two evils, so they would wait until the door was unlocked for them.

A very long night of fear seemed to last forever until finally they heard the key turn in the lock and the sister was there in front of them and telling them the coast was clear for them to go. She then noticed how pale and shaken they both looked and asked what was the matter. Still covered in the sweat of fear, they told her. They also told her they would never be coming back to room fourteen again. The sister's face became almost as white as theirs as she had visions of banknotes going into a bottomless black hole. The two lovers were both adamant that they would not return.

Once more room fourteen is quiet. It is still unused, but if anyone were to go into that room at midnight they would see a grey mist form into a woman.

THE NIGHT SISTER IS ARRESTED

Sister Henrietta Fortesque was feeling hot and bothered. She had been shopping and the day was really warm and humid. How she hated this sultry weather. Her throat felt parched, she had to have a drink. It was a toss-up whether she went to the café for a coffee or to the local for a shandy. The pub won. There was a chance she would be bought a drink in the bar, whereas if she went to the café she would have to buy her own.

It seemed very dark in the bar coming in from the bright sunlight outside. For a few seconds she could not see a thing. As soon as her eyes became adjusted to the darker light, she looked around the room to see if there was anyone she knew. There was not. However, luck seemed to be with her. A rather elegantly dressed man with a friendly smile upon his not bad-looking face asked if he might buy her a drink. She accepted, adding a whisky to the shandy she would have managed with, if she had been paying herself.

"Been doing a bit of shopping then?" he asked, trying to start up a conversation. "Yes," she replied, "but what a day I have picked for it." She did not bother to explain that it was the only day she could do her shopping with ease because tonight she was off duty. She finished her drink rather quickly and he insisted on buying her another, bringing out a big wad of twenty-pound notes and peeling one off to pay for it.

At the sight of the money, Sister Henrietta's eyes lit up. He seemed like a very nice man and if it made him happy to buy her another drink, why should she stop him. She toyed with the idea of telling him that she had lost her purse to see if he would offer some money to compensate for the loss, but she decided against the idea. There might be other ways of getting more from that bankroll, more than a tenner or two, which was all she could expect for her lost purse story.

Now her thirst was quenched her brain went into overdrive. Money always had that effect on her. She must not seem too eager. Perhaps if she strung him along for a bit, an idea would come to her. Her thoughts were rudely interrupted when he informed her that he would have to be going, as he had an appointment to keep. Could he give her a lift home first, if she did not live too far away? She thankfully agreed and as he carried her shopping to his car she was amazed and delighted to see that it was a top model Mercedes, the latest version. It signalled 'money' to her.

"I'm sorry I had to rush you," he apologised. "Perhaps I could make up for it by taking you out to dinner this evening. That is, if you have nothing else planned." That bankroll and the cost of that car meant he had to be quite well-to-do, so she accepted his invitation without any delay. They made arrangements to meet that evening.

She put her shopping away and then spent a leisurely hour soaking in a bubbly bath, dreaming of having so much money that she could afford to paper her walls with it. She spent the rest of that afternoon pampering herself and trying to figure out a way to get hold of that bankroll.

He called for her at 7.30 p.m. as promised. She felt quite elated when she saw the expensive car pull up outside her door. He was pleased when he saw how smart and attractive she looked. She wore a smart two-piece in a pale shade of blue with shoes to match. Hatless, her brunette hair set just the right contrast. She would be ideal for what he had in mind. He hoped his friend agreed. Unknown to Sister Henrietta she would be spied upon as they dined at 'The Ritz', a high-class restaurant in the town.

They had starters of asparagus rolled in smoked salmon, followed by lobster thermidor and finished with a fruit salad composed of fruits from around the world served with bowls of Devonshire cream. A liqueur coffee completed the two hours they had both enjoyed spending there.

He excused himself for a moment and went to the 'Gents'. There he met his friend as pre-arranged. He asked his friend what he thought of his dining companion. "She'll do," answered the thin, freckled-faced man. He had a mop of carroty red hair and seemed a rather untidy person. He seemed to lack everything that a woman would find attractive. He was as crafty as his pig-like eyes suggested.

"Right," said the elegant one. "Give me a few days to soften her up, then we will use her." Ginger said, "You'd better go now, you don't want to get in her bad books."

He returned to the table, apologising for being so long, then asked her if she would like to go on to a night-club he knew.

Henrietta began to have some unaccustomed feelings. She felt that this man, if anyone, was the man for her. Before, money was the only thing that could make her eyes sparkle but now this man was having the same affect. She wanted to feel his arms around her, wanted him to kiss and caress her. Yes, she admitted to herself, she wanted to give herself to him so they could both make mad, passionate love.

They entered the night-club, a posh, snobsville kind of place, went to a table and sat down. Almost immediately a waiter appeared at their side, as if by magic, and took their order. There was a small dance floor there which they tried out. After a few more drinks Henrietta wanted to go home, saying she was feeling tired.

In the car they kissed for the first time. It made Henrietta feel like a teenager. When they arrived at her house, she invited him in for a coffee. It was not long before the coffee cups were empty and her bed full.

For once Henrietta was not thinking about money, in fact the whole evening she had not thought about money. Now as they burned up energy together, she just wanted the ecstatic feeling to go on forever. They climaxed together and both lay back, panting slightly with their efforts. She felt great. He thought it was a hard way to make a living but it was better than working. They whispered sweet nothings to each other before falling asleep.

The next morning he awoke first and pottered around in the kitchen until he found everything needed to make coffee. He took a cup to her as she was still in bed. He asked her what time she had to get up for work, that is, if she went to work. He received a shock when he found out that she worked nights. He had another shock when he found out that she was a nursing sister, but his face gave nothing away. She asked him what sort of work he did. He told her he was a car dealer and his own boss, so he had no need to hurry back. She told him to come back to bed. They made love again, but this time far more sedately. Not a bit like the frenzy of the night. To her it was sheer poetry in motion.

Then, alas, it was time for him to leave. He made a date to see her in two days' time.

Because of the shocks he had received, he had to find his friend and make some adjustments to their usual arrangements. Ginger was seated at the bar of the Dog and Ferret, a pub situated in a town many miles from where he had met Henrietta, a place where he would never take her. After all, in his line of business he had to keep his tracks well covered. This was also the reason why Ginger and he were seldom seen together. They were on such a nice little earner, it paid to be careful. If things went wrong, which it sometimes did, in spite of all their careful planning, there was no lead back to either of them. This was the reason that they always used a third party to make their final transaction on any deal. The third parties were always well rewarded to avoid any spiteful comebacks. Very often the third parties did not even realise that they had been involved in criminal activities.

They stole high-class vehicles to order and sold them on to agents on the continent. The motor would be stolen in the U.K., altered and delivered to them. Technically they did not actually steal the cars themselves. The thieves, although they worked for them, never actually saw them.

Rather than risk taking the cars across themselves, the partners got the continental agents to pick them up from this country. Reducing the risk in this way cost them money but it did not really matter because they were still making plenty. This was where the third parties came in. The cars and cash were always exchanged through third parties. There was never any direct contact between them and those on the continent. The only people the continentals saw were the third parties, so if there were any slip-ups from there, there was no traceable link to them. The third parties were frequently changed and picked from various parts of the community and always from different areas. This was done as a security measure in case any third party became too inquisitive. No one in any part of the organisation could ever give their description to the authorities. This was probably the reason they had been in business for so long.

Ginger was not happy at having to alter their plans. It meant that they would have to change to a daylight exchange which made their operation more risky. He suggested they wait and find another third party. His partner disagreed. Among other things he fancied another bite at the cherry and he thought that, apart from the bind of having to alter the times, Henrietta would be ideal for the job. Besides they did not really have enough time to get a replacement — a delivery was expected in three days' time.

All that had to be done to complete the transaction now was for the third party to be at the pre-selected spot with the car to exchange it for a sealed envelope which would be handed over. (The third parties were told many and varied tales why this should be necessary.)

He kept his date with Henrietta. They had lunch at a local pub then made their way back to her house where they lost no time in getting into bed. She had had her doubts in the two days that she had waited to see him again, wondering if she had been right to let him go all the way on her first date. But she knew in her heart that she could never resist him. Now here he was with her again and all was well.

Her attitude at work had not altered. She was still the granite-faced boss of the night shift, and everyone knew it. But off duty she was now a totally different person. Her features softened even more as she cuddled the man in her bed.

He thought that now was the time to broach the subject of the reason for him being there, without of course giving too much away. "I'm in a bit of a fix," he said, as if by way of conversation. "I have to see two customers, both at the same time and neither will alter their times to suit me. This is the drawback of a one-man business." This was the first time he had mentioned to her it was only a one-man business. Somehow she had got the impression that he employed staff and had a showroom somewhere.

It was as if a sudden idea had hit him. "I wonder, I know it's a great cheek to ask after only knowing each other for such a short time, but I wonder if you can help me?" The way he looked at her, as he asked for help, she felt she could not refuse him anything.

"Of course I'll help you, if I can. But how?"

"If I leave you with the car — all the paperwork has been sorted — you could exchange the car and receive an envelope which will contain documents I require. Then I'll pick you up as soon as I have dealt with my other appointment." If she had not been so besotted by the man she might have thought this was a bit suspicious. As it was, she was only too pleased to do anything for him.

So there she was, in the middle of nowhere, all alone with only the car (top of the range model), waiting for the purchaser. She would be glad when it was all over. It seemed spooky waiting there.

A car appeared, travelling quite fast, and skidded to a stop beside her. An envelope was thrust into her hand and she jumped out of the car. One of the two men jumped into the driving seat she had just vacated and the two cars raced away. Not a word had been spoken. She thought this was a rather rum way of doing business, but before she could meditate further she was surrounded by police. She had no idea where they had sprung from. In the distance she could see the two cars being stopped by other police vehicles. The police cautioned her as she was arrested for dealing in stolen cars. She was speechless. How could she have been such a blind fool? That night she had her nightmare dream again, of all her money disappearing into a bottomless black hole.

The police, who had been tipped off by Interpol, had had the two car racketeers from the continent under surveillance from the moment they had entered the country.

When they saw the transaction taking place they started to move in. They thought they had caught one of the gang leaders as they met up with the hard-faced, well-dressed woman.

They did not believe her story. She had delivered the car, she had the money in her possession. Nevertheless they did hang around for an hour to see if anyone else turned up. Needless to say, the two major-domos this side of the Channel had got wind of the police being about and simply disappeared. The police questioned her for hours, but she had no surname, no address that she could give them. All she knew was that the man who had got her into all this was called Teddy.

Following her arrest, her employment at the nursing home was terminated, to the relief of everyone on the night shift there.